This book belongs to:

_ _ _ _ _ _ _ _

First published in Great Britain in 2015 by Andersen Press Ltd.,

20 Vauxhall Bridge Road, London SW1V 2SA.

Published in Australia by Random House Australia Pty.,

Level 3, 100 Pacific Highway, North Sydney, NSW 2060.

Colour separated in Switzerland by Photolitho AG, Zürich.

Printed and bound in Malaysia by Tien Wah Press.

British Library Cataloguing in Publication Data available.

ISBN 978 1 78344 160 0

10   9   8   7   6   5   4   3   2   1

Teddy Picnic

Georgie Birkett

Andersen Press

Everyone's excited,
everything is ready...

little hats and little shoes
for every little teddy.

Teddies walk, teddies skip, teddies on their way.

Teddies on a picnic trip...

Hip! Hip! HOORAY!

Teddies blowing bubbles
and hiding in the trees.

Teddies dancing in the woods
with butterflies and bees.

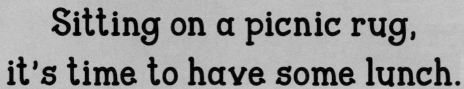

Sitting on a picnic rug,
it's time to have some lunch.

Lots of lovely things to eat...
Munch! Munch! Munch!

Teddies have full tummies,
so they run and play.

Birds land on the picnic rug
and take the crumbs away.

Happy teddies, sleepy teddies, time for home again.

Teddies' legs are tired so

teddies take the train!

Now teddies' hats and shoes come off, coming through the door.

The teddies are so tired,
they just **tumble** to the floor!

Climbing on the sofa, huddled in a heap,
teddies all agree it's time for books...

and sleep!